ATOS 2.6
AR pts 0.5
Lexile 500L

W9-BFN-214

DATE DUE

FAERIEGROUND

A Wish in the Woods

Book One

BY BETH BRACKEN AND KAY FRASER

ILLUSTRATED BY ODESSA SAWYER

STONE ARCH BOOKS

a capstone imprint

FAERIEGROUND IS PUBLISHED BY
STONE ARCH BOOKS
A CAPSTONE IMPRINT
1710 ROE CREST DRIVE
NORTH MANKATO, MINNESOTA 56003
WWW.CAPSTONEPUB.COM

LIBRARY OF CONGRESS CATALOGING-IN-
PUBLICATION DATA IS AVAILABLE ON THE
LIBRARY OF CONGRESS WEBSITE.

LIBRARY BINDING: 978-1-4342-3303-5

SUMMARY: SOLI AND LUCY ARE BEST
FRIENDS—UNTIL, ON FAERIE GROUND, SOLI
WISHES LUCY AWAY.

BOOK DESIGN BY K. FRASER
ALL PHOTOS © SHUTTERSTOCK WITH THESE
EXCEPTIONS: AUTHOR PORTRAIT © K FRASER
AND ILLUSTRATOR PORTRAIT © ODESSA
SAWYER

PRINTED IN THE UNITED STATES OF AMERICA
IN NORTH MANKATO, MINNESOTA.
012012
007144R

"*Wishes come true, not free.*"
– Stephen Sondheim, Into the Woods

For Valarie, who wished me away, and wished me home. -b
For the Fraser sisters: you are all a mother could wish for. -k

54629

Long ago, a kingdom was founded in Willow Forest . . .

The faerieground and human village weren't far from each other. They shared a dark wood. They shared the same sun, water, trees, and air. Visitors crossed the borders.

They were happy neighbors. At first. In the village, unrest was growing.

And in the faerieground, nothing was quite what it seemed.

Chapter 1

Soli

We are always together,

Lucy and I.

Lucy is the brave one. I am the fearful one.

We were born two weeks apart in different towns, and since then, we've always been together.

We are the kind of friends everyone wants. We are never apart. Her mother may as well be my mother. I spend hours at her house.

Lucy knows everything about me. Every detail of my life. And I know absolutely everything about her.

We are best friends. We do everything together. We always have. Or we did, anyway. We used to. Before.

We live in Mearston, a small town on the edge of Willow Forest. The trees in the woods are as old as trees can be. It's dark in there, dark and scary. Everyone says to stay out of the woods. Lucy's mother told her the woods were called the faerieground. She told us never to go there. She said that faeries lived there. She said if you made a wish in the woods, your wish would come true. That you'd wish you hadn't wished it.

We started going there when we were little
girls. We were three or four, roaming around
on our own. I didn't want to go in. But Lucy
said, "This will be our secret shortcut." It
made our walk to school half as long. So we
had extra time to play, to talk, to laugh, to be
together.

Lucy is not afraid of the woods. So neither am
I. Not anymore. But I'm careful there. I still
stay behind her. That's what best friends do.
They stay together.

Now we are thirteen. I still stay behind her.

Lucy has always led the way. She does everything first. She was born first. Our mothers tell us she walked first, talked first. Her first word was *sky*. Mine was *Lucy*.

She kissed a boy first. Last week.

I wouldn't care. I'd be happy for her. I'm used to her doing things first. I'm used to just being happy for her.

Except for one thing. It was Jaleel. He's the boy I like.

Jaleel is strong. He's smart. His smile is
amazing. Especially when he smiles at me. It's
like I know a secret about him that no one
in the world could guess. It's like we know
something secret about each other.

At school, I stay in shadowy corners, in dark
spaces. Lucy is out in the light. She's popular
and friendly and bold.

I am shy and quiet and hardly anyone knows
me, besides Lucy. I've never bothered to try to
get anyone else to know me.

When she's around, she puts everyone in the shadows. And I never mind. That's just who we are. Two sides of the same coin. Two halves of the same whole. She makes the light, and I stay in the dark.

But somehow, Jaleel saw me in the shadows. Lucy knew I liked him, and she kissed him anyway.

Then she told me about it. She said she was sorry. She said it just happened. She said it wouldn't happen again.

Of course, I believed her.

I thought I would forgive her. I thought she

was my best friend, and she'd never lie to me.

Then at school today, I saw them together.

I was walking through the crowds after lunch,

looking for Lucy. She was at her locker, fixing

her long, blond hair.

She's beautiful. Have I mentioned that? Lucy

is beautiful. I have always thought that she was

more beautiful than me.

But the thing about her is that you don't notice her beauty, because she's so kind, too. She's not one of those girls who is just pretty and nothing else.

Anyway. She was at her locker. Her hair looked perfect. The crowds parted.

I smiled and waved, but Lucy didn't see me. She wasn't looking my way. She was smiling up at someone else, someone taller. And the crowds parted more, and as everyone moved from between us I could see who the someone else was.

It was Jaleel. He leaned down and kissed her.

She stood up on her tiptoes, reaching for him.

That's when Lucy saw me.

Chapter 2

Lucy

Soli is like my sister.

All I want is to take care of her and make her happy. She spends so much time feeling bad, feeling dark, hiding away from everyone.

I wish she'd come out in the light like me. I wish she'd let people see how wonderful she is. I wish she could do that.

I love Soli. Like a sister. Except she's not my sister.

And here's the thing. Sometimes I think my mother likes Soli more than she likes me.

I know that's crazy. But ever since we were

born, Soli has spent hours and hours and hours

at my house.

I've watched them together.

My mother has fed her. My mother has bought

her clothes. My mother has dried her tears.

And my mother watches her.

Not in a creepy way. In a loving way. In a

careful way. In a protective way. In a way she

hardly ever looks at me.

As if Soli needs extra care. As if her own

mother is not enough. As if my mother needs

to take care of her too.

Or like I don't deserve as much care.

Sometimes I feel like I've left Soli behind.

Sometimes it feels like she doesn't like doing

the things I do. She's so quiet. She's so careful.

I like being loud and bright and full of life.

Once I had a party. I was ten. My mother

bought cake and sparklers. I didn't invite Soli.

I didn't even tell her about it.

When my mother found out, she cried. "She's

your best friend," my mother said.

She is. She is my best friend. She is like the

other half of me.

So of course I changed my mind. I invited Soli
to the party.

But is there anything wrong with wanting
something that could be just mine? Something
I wouldn't have to share with my best friend,
my sister?

My own mother? My own friends? My own
party?

My own boyfriend?

Does it make me a bad person?

She asked me to talk to Jaleel and I did. I talked to him. And I liked him. I didn't mean to. It just happened. Sometimes when you talk to someone, it just happens. You like them. And we kissed, and I told Soli about it, and I said I was sorry and that it would never happen again.

I thought it was true.

Then, at school today, she saw me kiss him again.

Chapter 3

Soli

After school, I run home through our shortcut in the woods.

I follow the path I know so well. I've never traveled it alone.

My backpack bounces against my back and my heart pounds. My feet stamp the ground.

I hear her voice. "Soli!" she calls. "Soledad! Wait! Stop, Soli, stop!"

I don't want to stop. So I keep going.

Right now, I feel like I never want to talk to Lucy ever again.

"Come on, Soli, wait up," she calls. "I mean it. Turn around! Let me talk to you. Please! Soli, please!"

In my head, I'm thinking *No, no, no.*

But my legs stop moving. I stand in the middle of Willow Forest, waiting for Lucy to catch up to me.

She grabs my hands, and I pull them away. She looks me in the eye, and I turn my face.

"Why did you lie to me?" I ask.

Lucy sits down on the grass. "I didn't mean to," she says. She pulls out stems of clovers and twists them in her long fingers. "I meant it when I said it wouldn't happen again. I didn't think he actually liked me."

"Maybe he doesn't," I say.

I want to hurt her feelings. I want to make her feel as bad, as stupid, as pathetic as she's made me feel.

How has this happened to us? How can I have these feelings of anger toward my best friend?

Lucy shrugs. "Maybe not," she tells me. "Maybe he doesn't really like me."

Then she looks up at me. She stands and pushes a string of flyaway hair away from my face. "But now I think I really like him. I'm sorry."

I feel tears crawling out of my eyes. One slips down my face. "How could you do that to me?" I ask.

"I know you like him," Lucy says softly. "And I know why."

"Why?" I ask.

"Because he's a nice guy," Lucy says. "Because he's nice to you. Because he notices you."

She's right about that. Jaleel notices me. And not in a bad way, either. And he is nice to me, nicer than any other boy I've ever known.

Once I was in the hallway and I tripped. I don't know how it happened. Maybe my shoe came untied. Maybe someone stuck their foot out on purpose. Maybe I just fell.

Oh, it was so embarrassing.

Sprawled on the floor, I felt my cheeks getting hot. I'm not used to people looking at me. Everyone saw. Everyone started to laugh.

Not Jaleel. He reached down and helped me up. Then he smiled at me and walked away.

Lucy would have helped me. But she wasn't there.

And now that I think about it, maybe she would have laughed too.

Now she sits in the woods, trying to apologize.

Trying to say she's sorry for liking a boy who's

likable. I should be able to understand.

"I understand that you're mad," she says.

"But —"

"No," I say. I shake my head.

Chapter 4

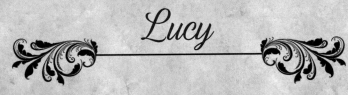

Lucy

Sometimes you hurt your
friends.

Sometimes you make your mother mad.

Sometimes you have to.

I guess today was my turn to hurt the person I love most in the world.

As soon as it happened, everything turned dark inside me. As soon as I saw Soli's dark eyes. I felt strange. I felt like a burned bowl of rose petals. I felt ruined.

I knew if I could take it back, I would.

I know I would.

When I chased her into the forest, I was also chasing myself. The good Lucy. Light Lucy. Lucy who makes her mother proud. Lucy who makes a mistake but fixes it.

When I finally invited Soli to the birthday party, the one I didn't want to tell her about, her eyes lit up. She didn't know everyone else had already been invited.

"It'll be so much fun!" she said.

I remember still, years later, exactly how her face looked. Full of hope. Full of trust. She wasn't surprised to be invited. She knew she belonged there.

And I felt terrible. I should have invited her first. I wasn't sure why I hadn't. I'm still not sure.

Sometimes friends start to feel like they aren't friends. Sisters feel like strangers.

Or maybe it was me who was changing.

After that, I was afraid to ever let Soli out of my sight. I didn't want to make my mother angry. And I was afraid of who I'd be without my other half.

Now, in the woods, Soli is angry with me. She should be. I kissed the boy she likes. I lied to her.

It's like the birthday party, except this time she found out, and I didn't have time to fix it. I couldn't make it all go away. I couldn't un-kiss Jaleel, and I'm not sure I would if I could.

"I understand that you're mad," I say, sitting

back down on the ground, pulling clovers,

counting leaves. "But—"

"No," Soli says.

We have been friends for thirteen years. We

will be friends for many more. She'll forgive

me. I know she will.

Inside I feel my light coming back.

Like the sun is rising.

Chapter 5

Soli

Once Jaleel and I walked home together.

Lucy was sick. I left school and took the long

way home. Soon I heard footsteps behind me.

"Wait up, Soli!" a voice said. It was Jaleel, and

he wanted to walk with me. And yes, I wanted

to walk with him too.

We talked about math class. We talked about

how the leaves crunch under your feet in the

fall. We talked about my dog and how he barks

at thunder.

I am not good at talking to people. But I was

good at talking to Jaleel.

Jaleel laughed every time I made a joke. We looked at each other and smiled. Sometimes we were quiet, but it didn't make me feel scared.

At a corner not far from my house, he stopped. "This is my street," he told me. "See you tomorrow."

"Okay," I said. "See you tomorrow." And I smiled, and I felt my face light up.

I went home feeling like I was holding a red-hot rose in my heart.

The next day I walked to school alone, the long way. I lingered by Jaleel's street, hoping he'd find me. He finally jogged down the block just as I was about to leave.

"Hey, Soli!" he said, slowing to a stop. "I'm so happy to see you."

"You are?" I asked. Then I smiled. "I'm happy to see you, too," I said.

We walked to school together. We talked the whole time.

When we were separating to walk to class, Jaleel asked if I was going to the basketball game.

"I hope you do," he said. "You should. You should come."

"I don't think I can," I told him.

I'd promised to help my mom with something. I don't remember what. But I knew I couldn't get out of it. Not for a basketball game.

I tried to hold tight to the rose in my chest.
He wanted me to go to the game. That was
enough for now.

After school, I walked home through the
woods with Lucy. I told her everything. All
about Jaleel. She knew who he was.

"I'm going to the game," she told me. "I'll talk
to him. See if he says anything about you. I'll
make this happen."

I waited all night. She finally called, late.

She'd been at the game. She sat by Jaleel. They talked. She mentioned me, and he said I was cool.

My heart heated up.

Then she stopped talking for a minute. There was more to the story.

After the game, while she waited for her dad to pick her up, Jaleel had kissed her. Or she had kissed him. She didn't know. Her voice shook as she told me.

"It was a total accident," she told me. "It didn't mean anything. I think he might like you!"

When I saw them in the hall today, the rose in my chest turned to coal.

Chapter 6

Soli

In the woods, I stare at my best friend.

"No," I say again.

"You're not mad?" Lucy asks, her face full of hope. "Oh, good!"

"No," I say. "I am mad. I'm really mad. Right now I just wish you weren't here."

A bright light bursts in the darkness of the forest. It blinds me. Then there's silence.

Just like that, Lucy is gone.

Chapter 7

Lucy

In the woods, Soli was angry.

I would have been angry too.

Wouldn't you? Your best friend kisses the boy you think you like—how would you feel? And imagine you're the friend who does the kissing. How would that feel? Who feels worse, the betrayed or the betrayer?

I feel like the worst friend ever.

I didn't mean to like him. I meant to get him to like Soli. When she talked about him, her face lit up.

Soli likes to be in the shadows. Jaleel made her feel light.

I wanted him to feel like that about her. But talking to him, and kissing him, his lips pressed against mine—that made me feel light as air and twice as bright. I forgot about Soli.

Would Soli have forgotten about me?

If it was the other way around. What would she have done?

Would she have kissed him back?

In the woods, when she was angry, Soli made a wish.

As long as Soli and I have been coming to the woods, I've been trying to keep her from wishing. The woods can't hurt you if you don't wish. Anyone who believes in faeries knows that.

But I never let Soli believe in them, in the faeries. That was the one thing I did to keep her safe. My one protection. I told her my mother's stories were just that. Stories.

Her mother wasn't from here. She had no

reason to believe. Her mother hadn't heard the

stories her whole life. Not like my mother.

The faeries keep their distance. It hasn't been

easy. And if Soli ever said, "I wish——" I would

change the subject or interrupt her.

This time I didn't.

And she wished me away.

Away to the fairieground.

Chapter 8

Lucy

My whole life, my mother has
left the faeries offerings.

She leaves the gifts at the edge of the woods. Pinned butterflies. Dried lavender. Mushrooms. Rosemary. A small jar of honey. Every time the season changes, she brings them something.

I never go along with her when she leaves these presents. She goes alone, before dawn. The only reason I know is because once I followed her.

Once, I asked her why.

"I angered the queen," she whispered.

It was dark and we sat in lawnchairs in our

backyard. Here and there, a firefly sparked.

She reached up to her neck and tangled her

fingers in her necklace. She wouldn't tell me

anything more. I didn't dare ask.

Chapter 9

Lucy

The faeries aren't how I imagined them.

I thought they'd be pretty, maybe sweet, tricky.

I sort of thought they'd be like me.

The faeries are darker than I imagined. More

beautiful. Scarier. Meaner.

One of the faeries, a strong one, comes over to

me in the clearing. Her voice is like a broken

glass bell.

"Lucy," she says. "The light one."

"Why am I here?" I ask, even though I know

already.

She sneers at me. I look down at my body. My clothes are dirty. Leaves linger in my hair. For the first time, I feel afraid.

"You're here because your friend wished you away," she tells me.

I try to stand, but my hands are laced to the ground by braids of grass. "How can I leave?" I ask. "Does she just need to wish me back home?"

Soli, I think. *Wish me home. Please.*

The dark faerie shakes her head. "You're not the one the queen wants," she says. "She wants the dark one. The scared one. The lonely one. The other one."

"Soli?" I ask.

"Yes," the faerie says. "She needs Soledad to do something. A favor. When she's done it, you'll be free."

"What if she doesn't want to do it?" I ask. "This favor for the queen."

The faerie laughs. "Well, forever is a long time," she says.

"How will she know what to do?" I ask.

The faerie laughs again. "We'll send her a message," she tells me.

Chapter 10

Soli

Lucy is gone.

I can't sleep. I don't know what happened.

Have the stories come true? The stories about

wishing in the woods, about the faeries, all

those silly stories her mother's always told?

They can't be true.

There are no faeries. Not in this world.

At midnight, a rock shatters my window. A leaf

is wrapped around it. I am afraid to touch it.

I am afraid to stand near the broken shards of

glass.

There are words scratched into the rock in

angry letters. I can't read them.

The only one I know is *Lucy*.

Find out what's next . . .

FAERIEGROUND

FAERIEGROUND

The Shadows

by Beth Bracken and Kay Fraser   Illustrated by Odessa Sawyer

Step out of the shadows.

Soledad and Lucy are best friends, but they aren't the same. Lucy is loud and social; Soli is quiet and solitary. Lucy is outgoing and brave, but Soli prefers quiet and safety. Lucy is active, driving their lives, and Soli lets her be. Light follows Lucy, but Soli— Soli keeps to the shadows.

Now Lucy is locked in a faerie dungeon with only the company of Kheelan, a faerie revolutionary. She can't take action. The argument that made Soli wish her there has to be put aside. For the first time in their lives, Soli has to take a step out of the shadows and save her friend.

Beth & Kay

Kay Fraser and Beth Bracken are a designer-editor team in Minnesota.

Kay is from Buenos Aires. She left home at eighteen and moved to North Dakota—basically the exact opposite of Argentina. These days, she designs books, writes, makes tea for her husband, and drives her daughters to their dance lessons.

Beth and her husband live in a tiny, crowded bungalow with their son, Sam, and their Jack Russell terrier, Harry. She spends her time editing, reading, daydreaming, and rearranging her furniture.

Kay and Beth both love dark chocolate, Buffy, and tea.

Odessa

Odessa Sawyer is an illustrator from Santa Fe, New Mexico. She works mainly in digital mixed media, utilizing digital painting, photography, and traditional pen and ink.

Odessa's work has graced the book covers of many top publishing houses, and she has also done work for various film and television projects, posters, and album covers.

Highly influenced by fantasy, fairy tales, fashion, and classic horror, Odessa's work celebrates a whimsical, dreamy and vibrant quality.